# By the Sea

## by Anne Welsh Guy

### illustrated by
### Wendell Kling

WHITMAN PUBLISHING COMPANY
Racine, Wisconsin
Printed in the U.S.A. by Western Printing and Lithographing Company

Toward evening,
    as the western sky
    was turning beautiful colors,
    Stephen walked down to the sea.
His grandfather walked with him.
Stephen carried his pail and scoop.
He carried his very bravest lead soldier.
Grandfather had his pipe.

Across the white sand they went
    toward the sea.
They were alone,
    except for the tall shadows
    that walked before them,

And for a fisherman
    standing near the point
    where the lighthouse was.
He stood still as a statue
    with his fishline
    cast into the rolling surf.

On the edge of the shore
    little sandpipers on tiny stick legs
    ran to meet the waves
    as the tide washed
    in and out.
A big ship sailed
    slowly, far out at sea.
They heard its dull
    deep voice.

Stephen splashed
   his bare feet
   in the lacy edges of
   white foam.
Grandfather rolled up
   his trouser legs.
He puffed some big puffs on his pipe.

The water was not as cold
   as it had been that morning.
Stephen felt glad and excited.
Grandfather was with him,
   exploring with him
   by the sea at evening time.
They were exploring together,
   by the sea at evening time,
   all alone together.

Now the sun was a great ball
   in the western sky,
   a great golden ball.
Flocks of gray sea gulls flew overhead.
   "Waak, waak," they cried
   as they glided and flapped their wings.
They dipped to the waves,
   searching for fish
   for their evening supper.

Stephen and Grandfather
   knelt on the sand.
They saw many tiny holes,
   like polka dots,
   all over the sand.
The skeletons of little sand bugs
   were scattered all about.
The mighty ocean had caught the sand bugs,
   had caught and battered and broken them
   before they could climb
   into their tiny holes.
Little white skeletons lay all over the sand.

Stephen and Grandfather
   walked down the shore
   toward the lighthouse.
The tide was coming in.
A wave swirled over their feet.
As the water ran back into the sea,
   Stephen picked up shells
   and looked at them.
He put some of the shells into
   his pail.

One shell
was like
a lady's fan.

One was like
a horn.

There were
shells
that were
like black
boats,

And heart-shaped cockles,

And a big whelk shell
that whispered a
song of the sea as
Stephen held it
to his ear.

On a part of the sand that was wide and hard,
Stephen and Grandfather stopped
and wrote their names with a driftwood
stick.

Stephen built a
 fort around the names,
 to keep them safe from the sea.
He set his lead soldier
 to guard the fort,
 his very bravest soldier.

Then the surf came up in a great wave.
It washed their names away.
Before Grandfather or Stephen could save him,
    it washed the lead soldier away.
The soldier was washed into the sea.

Stephen was sad.
He had lost his very bravest lead soldier.
Tears ran down his cheeks.
Grandfather wiped the tears away
    with a big handkerchief.

Water from the sea almost covered
the beach now.
The golden sun had dropped behind the sand.
Gray mist was everywhere.
Lights began to show
in the little beach houses.

From the lighthouse, a beacon began to flash—
    on and off . . . on and off—
    sending its beams across the waves.
The fisherman reeled in his line,
    gathered up his pail,
    and walked away.
Grandfather and Stephen turned toward home.

Suddenly it became very dark.
Only the light from the lighthouse,
    and the friendly smiling faces
    of the lighted cottages,
    and, far out at sea,
    the tiny twinkling lights of unseen ships
    showed in the dark night.
Stephen slipped his hand into Grandfather's.
Grandfather took out his big flashlight.
He flashed its cheerful light on
    the sand in front of them.

And then they saw the fiddler crabs!
Dozens and dozens of little fiddler crabs,
    who like to come out when it gets dark,
    were scurrying as the light was turned
    on them.
The crabs went hurrying into their holes
    with their funny sideways walk.
Grandfather stooped down
    and picked up a crab.

Stephen looked at the funny little face.
The crab's eyes stuck out
        as though on sticks.
When the light shined on his face,
        the crab pulled his eyes back
        as though he were afraid.
He held his big "fiddler" claw up
        and waved it
        as if he were trying to protect himself.

For a time, Stephen and Grandfather watched
the fiddlers dig their long deep holes.
They watched them hurry into their holes
whenever a wave came washing toward them
and come running back out
as the wave rolled back.

A big wave came rolling in,
    a very big wave.
And as the wave ebbed away,
    and the fiddlers ran out,
    Stephen saw something.

His little lead soldier lay on the sand!
Right among the fiddlers he lay,
    looking up at Stephen.
    The sea had sent him back!

With a glad cry, Stephen ran
to pick up his soldier.
He put him deep in his pocket
and did not let him go.

A bell clanged loud and clear.
It was the bell that was kept near the door
of Stephen's cottage.
Mother was ringing the bell.
It was suppertime.

With the flashlight to guide them,
Stephen and Grandfather went hand in hand
across the sand and through the black night
toward the cottage.

They smelled the good smell
    of crisp fish frying
    as they came to the cottage door.
They saw Mother's smiling face
    and they stepped into the cheerful
    lighted house.
Daddy gave Stephen a great big bear hug,
    and they all sat down at the table.

They bowed their heads.
"Thank you for this happy family,
    for the good fish to eat," Daddy said.
Stephen put his hand in his pocket.
He felt of the little lead soldier
    safe and deep in his warm pocket.

Outside the cottage door,
   the beach was all alone.
A pale new moon came up
   and made a faint rippling light on the water.
The beach was dark and still.
There was no sound,
   except the voice of the sea,
   the steady pounding voice of the sea,
   as the waves lapped against the shore.